# Goldilocks
### and
# The Three Bears

Retold by Heather Amery

Illustrated by Stephen Cartwright

Language consultant: Betty Root

Series editor: Jenny Tyler

There's a li n every page.

The Three Bears live in a forest.

There's great big Father Bear, there's middle-sized Mother Bear, and there's tiny wee Baby Bear.

Mother Bear fills three bowls with porridge.

But it's too hot to eat. "We'll go for a walk while it cools,"
says Father Bear. And they go out of the cottage.

Along comes a naughty girl called Goldilocks.

She peers through the cottage window. She sees there's no one at home. She opens the door and looks in.

She sees the bowls of porridge.

She tries them all. "That one's too hot," she says. "That one's too cold. This one is just right," and she eats it all up.

Goldilocks feels sleepy.

She sits on Father Bear's chair. "That's too hard," she says.

"That's too soft," she says, trying Mother Bear's chair.

She sits on Baby Bear's chair.

"This is just right," she says, and goes to sleep. There's a crack. The chair breaks and she falls on the floor.

Goldilocks goes into the bedroom.

She lies on Father Bear's bed. "That's too high," she says. She tries Mother Bear's bed. "That's too low," she says.

She lies on Baby Bear's bed.

"This is just right," she says. Soon she is fast asleep. She doesn't hear the Three Bears come into the cottage.

The Bears want their breakfast.

Father Bear says, "Who's been eating my porridge?" Mother Bear says, "Who's been eating my porridge?"

Baby Bear looks at his bowl.

"Who's been eating my porridge? And they've eaten it all up," he says. And he starts to cry big tears.

"Someone's been in here," says Father Bear.

He looks around the room. Then he looks at his chair. "Who's been sitting in my chair?" he says.

Mother Bear looks at her chair.

"Who's been sitting in my chair?" she says. "Who's been sitting in my chair, and broken it?" says Baby Bear.

The Three Bears go into the bedroom.

"Who's been sleeping in my bed?" says Father Bear.

"Who's been sleeping in my bed?" says Mother Bear.

Baby Bear looks at his bed.

"Who's been sleeping in my bed?" he says, "And, look, she's still in it." Goldilocks wakes up, very scared.

# Goldilocks jumps out of bed.

She jumps out of the window and runs home to her mother.
The Three Bears never, ever see her again.

This edition first published in 2003 by Usborne Publishing Ltd, 83-85 Saffron Hill, London EC1N 8RT, England. www.usborne.com
Copyright © 2003, 1996 Usborne Publishing Ltd.